For my sister Iris,
who always helps me make the right ones

First published in 2021 by Child's Play (International) Ltd. Ashworth Road, Bridgemead, Swindon SN5 7YD, UK

First published in USA in 2021 by Child's Play Inc. 250 Minot Avenue, Auburn, Maine 04210

Distributed in Australia by Child's Play Australia Pty Ltd. Unit 10/20 Narabang Way, Belrose, Sydney, NSW 2085

ISBN 978-1-78628-564-5
SJ260221CPL04215645

Printed in Shenzhen, China

1 3 5 7 9 10 8 6 4 2

A catalogue record of this book is available from the British Library

www.childs-play.com

CHOICES

Roozeboos

Life is full of choices.

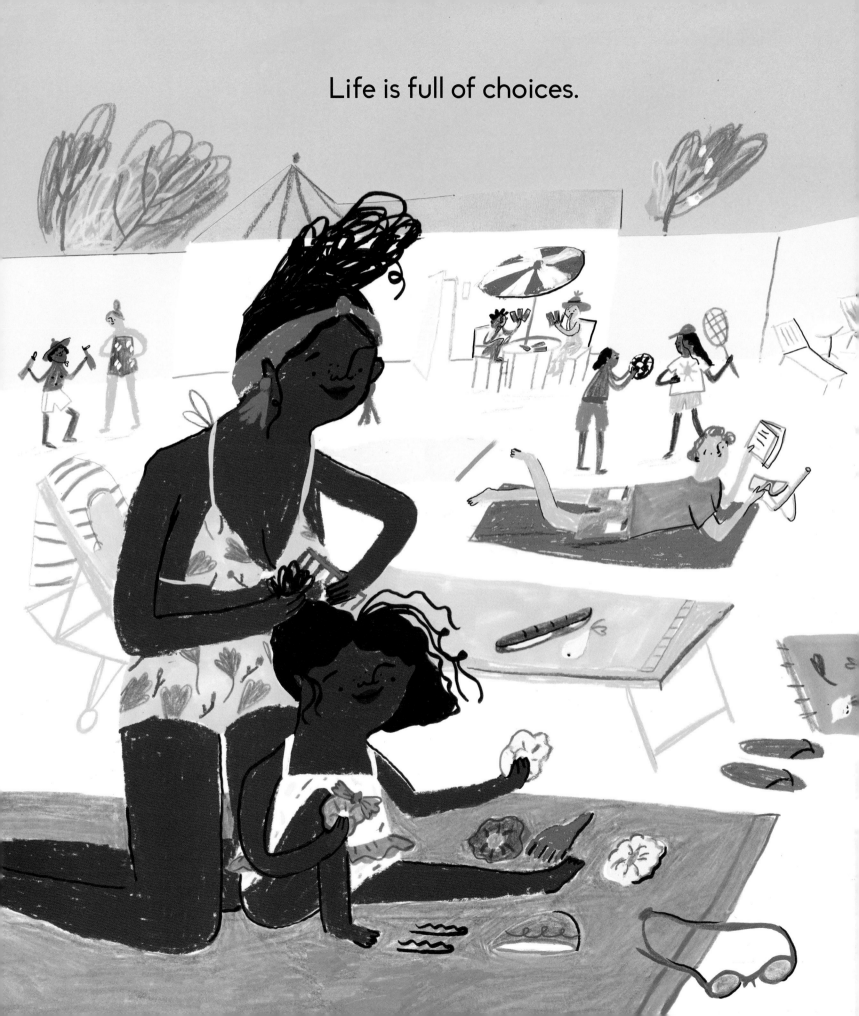

You can find them everywhere!

They can be little choices...

or bigger ones.

You can choose to stand out...

or to blend in
with the others.

You can go wild...

or just take it easy.

You can choose to be very careful...

Some choices...

are easy to make.

But other choices...

take a bit more time.

But when you're ready,

and it all feels right,

just follow your heart!

Life is full of choices...

and with every choice you grow!